W9-ABJ-301

RECEIVED
MAY 09 2013
By

Saturday with Daddy

Dan Andreasen

Christy Ottaviano Books
Henry Holt and Company
New York

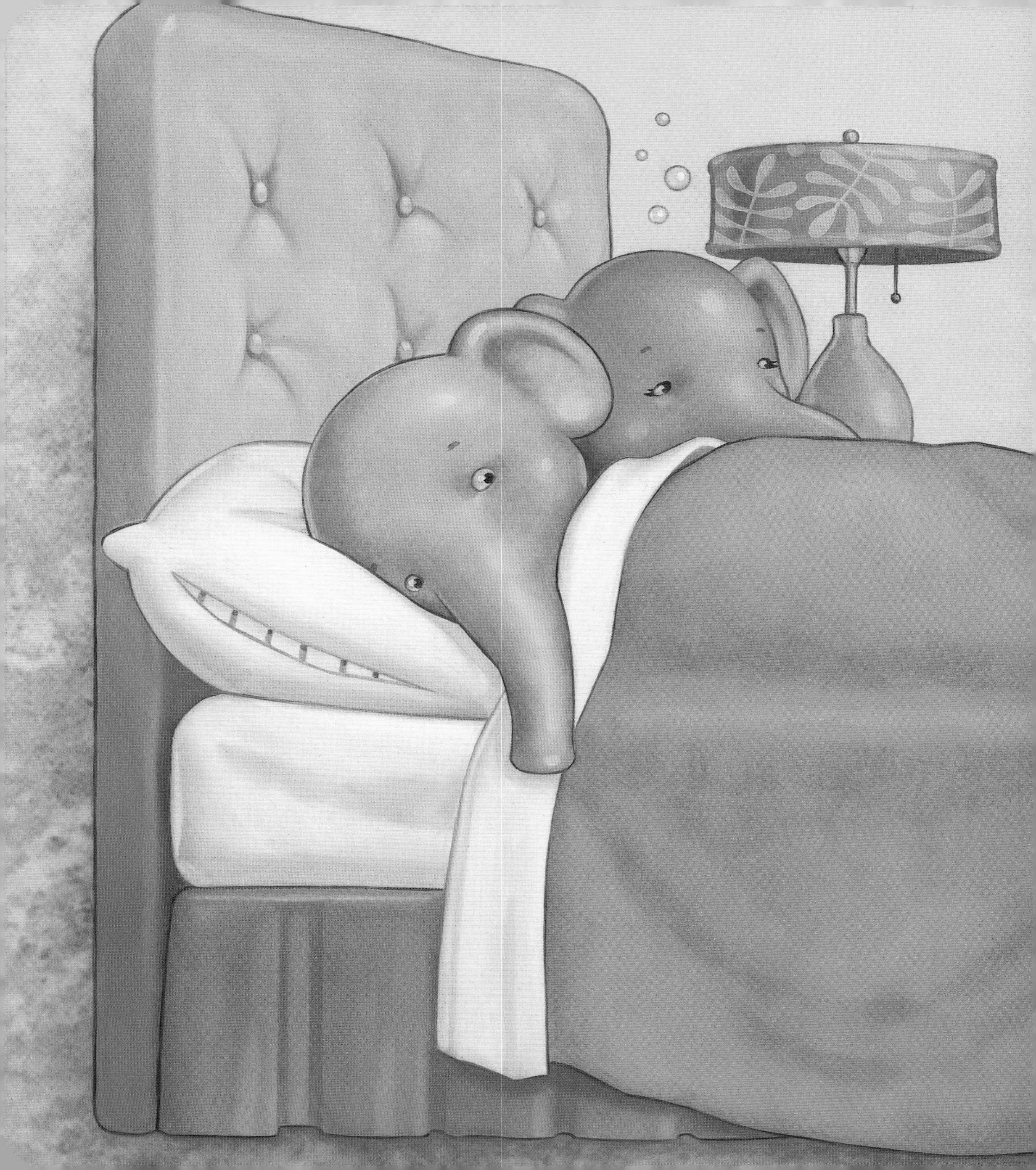

Saturday morning I'm always the first to wake up.

Rise and shine!

When Mommy and Daddy get up, the whole house smells like coffee.

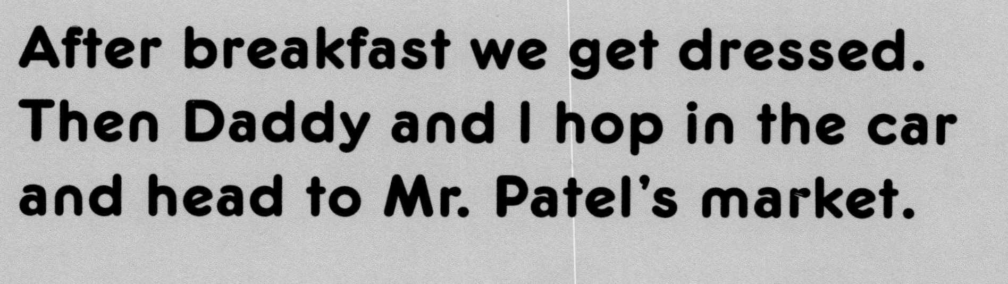

After breakfast we get dressed. Then Daddy and I hop in the car and head to Mr. Patel's market.

We sing along to our favorite songs on the radio.

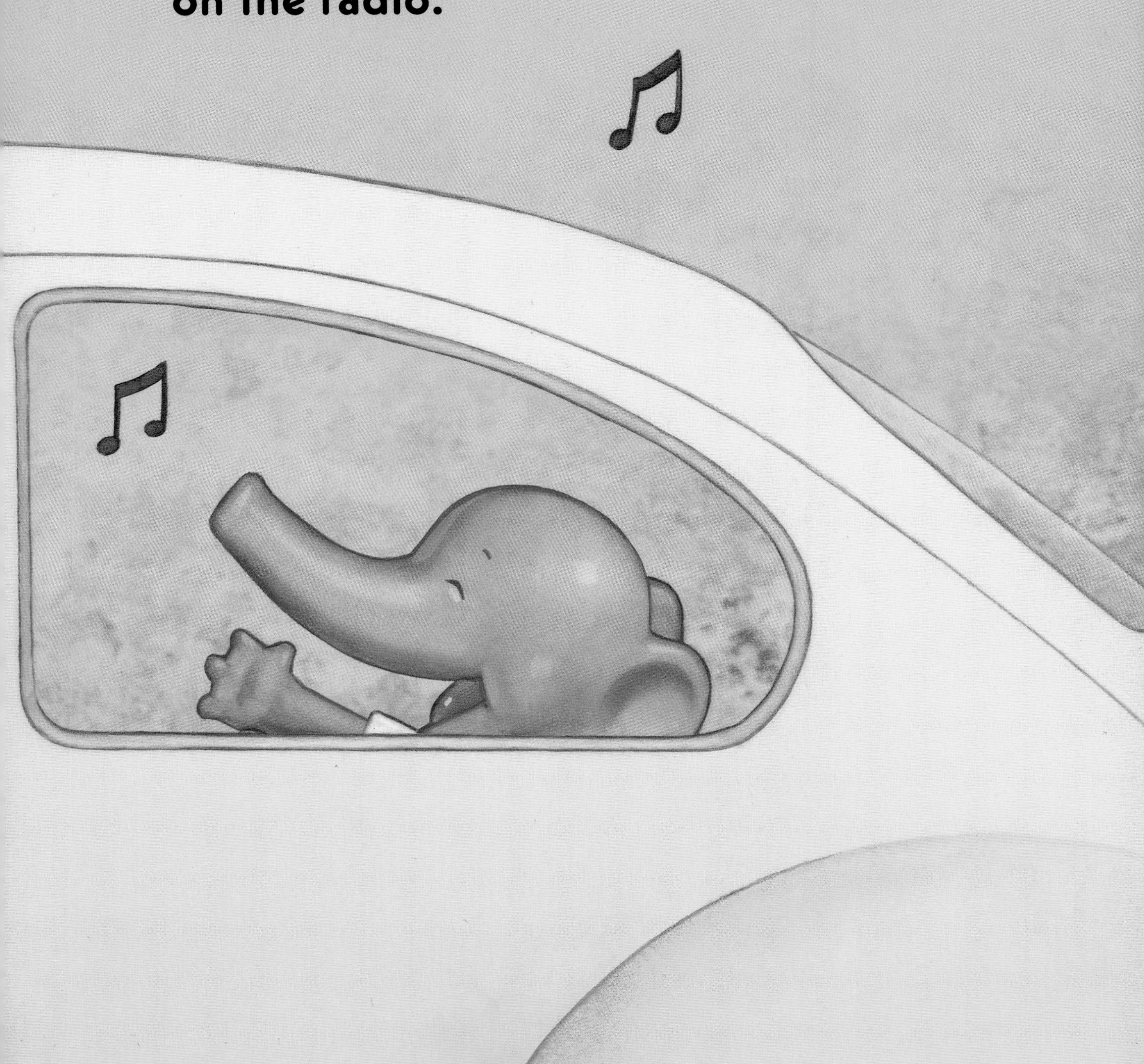

We buy marshmallows and hot dogs
and a great big bag
of charcoal.

We're going to have a cookout!

The next stop is Handy's Hardware Store.

I like the shiny red barbecue grill the best.

When we return home, Daddy needs my help. I hold the heavy wrench as Daddy turns the screws that put together the new grill.

On Saturday I wear the same kind of apron that Daddy wears.

Mommy makes a tray of deviled eggs that look like tiny white and yellow boats.

The best thing about
eating in the backyard
is not having to worry
if I spill something.

After lunch, Daddy stirs up the dusty coals so I can toast marshmallows.

Later, we toss the Frisbee around.

I try to catch it
but mostly miss.

"Nap time," Mommy says . . .

. . . so we pile into the big hammock.

Saturday with Daddy
is my best day
of the week!